W9-BZY-171

M & M

and the
Halloween Monster

By Pat Ross

Pictures by Marylin Hafner

Viking

VIKING
Published by the Penguin Group
Viking Penguin, a division of Penguin Books USA Inc.,
375 Hudson Street, New York, New York 10014, U.S.A.
Penguin Books Ltd, 27 Wrights Lane, London W8 5TZ, England
Penguin Books Australia Ltd, Ringwood, Victoria, Australia
Penguin Books Canada Ltd, 10 Alcorn Avenue, Toronto, Ontario, Canada M4V 3B2
Penguin Books (N.Z.) Ltd, 182–190 Wairau Road, Auckland 10, New Zealand

Penguin Books Ltd, Registered Offices: Harmondsworth, Middlesex, England

First published in 1991 by Viking Penguin, a division of Penguin Books USA Inc.
1 3 5 7 9 10 8 6 4 2
Text copyright © Pat Ross, 1991
Illustrations copyright © Marilyn Hafner, 1991
All rights reserved
Library of Congress Catalog Card Number: 91-50294
ISBN 0-670-83003-8
Printed in the United States of America
Set in Times Roman

For Ryan, David, and Alex

Chapter One
October Shivers

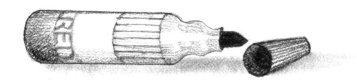

Mandy and Mimi, the friends M and M, flipped to a new page of Mandy's big wall calendar.

It said OCTOBER, a month that always gave the friends chills and shivers. Quickly, the friends looked for the square that said "31."

Mandy found a bright red marker. "For blood," she said. "Really red blood." Mimi found a green marker they never used. "For slime," she said. "A gross green for slime." Then they took turns writing *hallo* in blood and *ween* in slime.

"We'll make our own costumes like always," said Mandy, excited now. "We'll make marshmallow ghosts and eat them, and we'll carve really scary pumpkins."

"Yeah!" cried Mimi. "And we'll have cider and donuts at school. And no homework that night. We'll get tons of candy. And we won't get sick like last year," she added.

"We'll trick-or-treat EVERYBODY in our building!" cried Mandy.

"Everybody?" asked Mimi, who wondered if her friend had forgotten.

Suddenly Mandy remembered—like a bad dream. There were a few people the friends would not be trick-or-treating this year. Or any year.

First, there was mean Mrs. Haite who was just like her name. She liked to report M and M for riding the elevator up and down and pushing all the buttons.

No, they would not trick-or-treat that old witch on Halloween.

They would not trick-or-treat the man who had a dog named Godzilla. Godzilla drooled a lot and showed his pointy teeth when he saw M and M in the lobby. No, they would not be a tasty trick or treat for that beast on Halloween.

They would not trick-or-treat the woman upstairs who smelled like cafeteria hot dogs. Even the hallway on her floor smelled like dead things. No, they would not trick-or-treat that mummy on Halloween.

Just the thought of all the creepy
people living in their very own
apartment building began to spoil the
fun of Halloween.

To make themselves feel better, the
friends decided to make Krispie
Treats. The recipe was on the cereal box.

The treats were delicious, but the kitchen was one sticky mess!

"We have to dump this stuff before my mom comes home," Mandy said.

Everyone in the building had to take their trash to the end of the hall by the back stairs. Then Fred the handyman took it away.

Mimi opened the door and Mandy carried the trash. Together they headed down the hall. Maxi followed the bag.

Just ahead, where the hallway led to the back stairs, Mandy and Mimi saw a shadowy figure disappear down the stairs. The only sound they heard was the rattling of chains. At first they thought it was Fred the handyman.

But Fred always stopped to joke with them.

When they got to the stairs, they saw bright red drops of something on the floor. "Blood!" they cried. They could still hear the chains clanking on the stairs below. Without a word, they dropped the trash and raced home! Maxi barked all the way.

"It disappeared," said Mimi, remembering the figure by the stairs.

"Ghosts like to do that," said Mandy. "Halloween might be thirty-one days away, but things are already getting creepy."

They ate the Krispie Treats with milk and tried to forget about Halloween.

Chapter Two
Creepy Cages

Every year, the building where Mandy and Mimi lived had a Halloween party in the lobby right after dinner. And every year, there was a prize for the Best Costume. A lot of the kids wore store-bought costumes, but M and M didn't want to look like everybody else. And they both wanted to win the prize.

"I'm going to be a princess bride," announced Mandy without being asked.

"But you were a bride last year," groaned Mimi.

"I was a *plain* bride last year," Mandy corrected. "This is the princess kind."

Mimi had her own ideas about good costumes. "I'm going as a credit card," she announced.

"What a great idea!" cried Mandy. "I'll bet nobody thinks of that one." Suddenly, Mandy hoped that being a princess bride didn't seem dumb. A credit card was really smart.

Mandy needed something lacy and white for her costume. She remembered a pair of old white curtains that her mother put away in the basement.

Mimi needed something flat and hard. She remembered a big poster board left over from a project for art. It was downstairs now, in the basement.

The apartment building where Mandy and Mimi lived had a big storage room in the basement. The room had spaces there called cages because they were made with wire and you could walk right into them. The door to each cage was locked with a padlock. People could store things there like bikes and old furniture and rusty high chairs.

It was like having a messy attic if you lived in a house. That was the good thing.

The bad thing about cages was that they were in the basement.

Mandy and Mimi didn't mind the basement when people were waiting in the laundry room for their clothes to be finished. It was noisy and friendly then.

But this was a beautiful Sunday and everyone would be out in the park. No one would be doing laundry then. Still, they wanted to get started.

"It's quiet down here," said Mimi when they got to the basement.

"Too quiet," whispered Mandy. "And too dark!"

They walked down the long dark
hallway that led to the big storage
room. When they got to the entrance,
Maxi refused to go one more step.

"Do you think Maxi knows
something we don't, and should?"
wondered Mandy out loud.

The door to the cage room was heavy,
and it took both of them to push it open.

The cages were numbered.
Unfortunately, Mandy's cage number 20
was in the very back. Mimi's number
22 was right across from Mandy's.

Mandy's padlock was rusty but the
key worked. The big cage door
creaked like a prison.

Mandy found the box with the curtains right away. But the curtains were not very white anymore, and not as pretty as she had remembered. She wouldn't look like a princess bride. She'd look like some old window!

"Don't worry. We'll find something else," Mimi said to cheer up her friend.

Together Mandy and Mimi went through stuffed animals and old dolls, strollers and bicycle tires, fans and pots and pans . . . until they came across Mandy's pink tutu from ballet class.

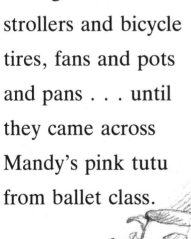

"A strawberry milkshake!" cried Mimi. She put the pink tutu on Mandy's head like a crown. "You can wear your pink sneakers and your mom's pink sweatshirt. And you can put the tutu on your head. Then you'll be a delicious strawberry shake!"

"Anyone can be a bride," agreed Mandy. "Nobody else will think of this!"

In Mimi's cage, the friends had to move dusty boxes and some old porch furniture to get to the cardboard. Maxi liked all the junk because there were more hiding places. He picked a big camp trunk.

Mandy and Mimi were ready to get out of there when they heard the heavy door to the storage room groan as it opened. Suddenly, they knew they were not alone.

"Move over, Maxi!" they whispered. From behind the camp trunk, the friends had a good view. They had a good view of a shadow on the wall growing larger and larger as it came closer and closer.

The shadow was monster-like. Its powerful shoulders were hunched over. And it was struggling to hold something round under one arm and drag a heavy bag with the other.

"A monster!" whispered Mandy. For once, Mimi had to agree.

The lights were dim, but they could see that the monster was headed for cage number 13.

"That figures," groaned Mimi. "Number thirteen is the right place to hide a body all right. And a head that goes with the body."

"Maybe we've been watching too much TV," whispered Mandy.

"We'd better split while we can still get away," whispered Mimi. "I just hope it doesn't have supersonic vision."

Mandy grabbed Maxi so tight he couldn't bark. Then the two friends ran for the door so fast that their footsteps made the cages rattle.

"Hello!" cried the monster as they passed cage number 13. "Wait!" they could hear it say as they jumped into the elevator and hit the button for "2."

"It tried to sound human!" cried Mandy. "To fool us."

"It knows who we are," cried Mimi. "We'll never be safe in this building again."

Chapter Three
Costume Secrets

The next week Mandy and Mimi tried to forget about a monster in the basement, a body in a bag, and a horrible head in cage number 13. Instead they started to work on their Halloween costumes.

Mandy found a pink sweatshirt in her mother's closet and borrowed it. She glued cotton balls to an old pair of shoes that were tight in the toes. The cotton would look like the whipped cream that drips down the glass.

Mimi's credit card costume needed a lot of work. She cut one cardboard square for the front and one for the back. She painted both sides with silver paint.

Mimi borrowed her mother's credit card to copy the numbers onto the front of her costume. Then she decorated her card with stars and rainbows. She gave her card a name, too. BIG SPENDER CARD. And she wrote *Mimi* carefully in the name space on the back.

The friends had gotten off to a very good start.

The day before Halloween, Mandy and Mimi decided to check their costumes.

"Mine needs green," complained Mimi. "Green is the color of money, and this costume is missing green. With all this silver, people will think I'm a tinfoil baking pan with numbers."

"Ski tights," said Mandy, pulling on her bright pink ballet tights. "My mom has very green ski tights that would fit you. They're the color of money. And they're with our ski stuff down in the basement."

The basement! Mandy had let the awful word slip.

So the friends M and M set out for the place they most dreaded just one more time.

Luckily, it was a rainy Sunday. The basement was filled with people doing laundry. The heat from the clothes dryers made it feel cozy and safe.

They passed cage number 13 without saying a word. They found the green tights right away. They headed for the door.

"There's nobody here but us," said Mimi, curious about cage number 13.

"Nobody but a body in a bag, and a head that needs a body," said Mandy who just wanted to leave.

"It will only take a second to check it out," said Mimi, pulling Mandy toward cage number 13.

Cage number 13 was quiet—too quiet. The bag was a lump now in the very back where they could not see it well.

There were stains on the floor where the monster had tried to wipe up the blood. A wooden crate—just the right size for trapping small children—had dribbles of blood the monster had missed.

"Just as I expected," cried Mimi. "It's the monster's hiding place."

The lights flickered and dimmed.

"This is not my idea of a good time!" cried Mimi, who headed for the door. Mandy was close behind.

The elevator took forever to come. When the doors opened, Mandy and Mimi pushed their way inside and bumped right into a boy who was getting off.

Mandy and Mimi knew everyone who lived in their building, but they didn't know this new kid. He was walking a bicycle toward the cages.

"Do you think we should tell him?" asked Mandy.

"He'll find out soon enough," answered Mimi, as the elevator doors shut and they headed safely home.

28

Chapter Four
The Trick

Halloween was turning into a horror show for Mandy and Mimi. Mandy decided to make a list of all the creepy things they had seen and heard:

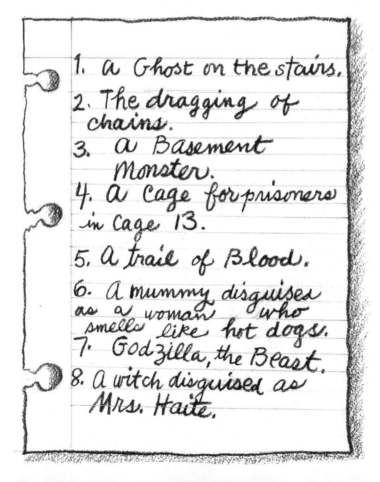

1. A Ghost on the stairs.
2. The dragging of chains.
3. A Basement Monster.
4. A cage for prisoners in Cage 13.
5. A trail of Blood.
6. A mummy disguised as a woman who smells like hot dogs.
7. Godzilla, the Beast.
8. A witch disguised as Mrs. Haite.

Then she added:

9. A Strange New boy!

"He looked normal," said Mimi.

"But things aren't the same this year," said Mandy. "For all we know, he could be the monster's son."

"Let's just skip Halloween," suggested Mimi. Mandy agreed.

But Mandy and Mimi changed their minds when they came home from school on October 31. The halls were already filled with little kids dressed up, shouting "Boo!"

People who wanted trick-or-treaters hung a special pumpkin sign on their front doors. After dinner, everyone got together in the lobby for a party. That's when they gave out the prizes.

In all the excitement, Mandy and Mimi forgot to forget about Halloween.

They dressed fast. Mimi's ski tights were a little big and a little hot, but the green was good. Mandy used her mother's lipstick—called Bright Berries—on her lips, her cheeks, and the tip of her nose.

Maxi was sitting by the door, waiting for trick-or-treaters. No one was paying attention to him. Suddenly, he let out a howl that sounded like a song.

"A rock star!" cried Mimi. "Maxi wants to be a rock star."

It didn't take long to fix up Maxi. First, they gave him a diamond neck band. Then they put sticky hair stuff all over his fur and made it punk and

spiky. Finally, the three were ready
for a quick dinner, and then the party
in the lobby.

"Have some punch, girls!" Mrs. Haite
called to them when they got there.

"It's probably poison," said Mandy.

But the punch tasted sweet and
cold. And Mrs. Haite offered them
seconds. She didn't act like a witch at all.

Maxi was a hit with everyone, including Godzilla. Now Maxi and his new friend rolled an apple around the lobby floor. That nasty dog was acting more like a kitten than a beast.

The smelly woman from upstairs was in charge of bobbing for apples. That game was the friends' favorite.

"Hold your nose," moaned Mimi.

But close up the woman smelled like fresh baby powder and roses. Not like a mummy at all.

"The contest is next," whispered Mandy. "You'll win."

"No, you'll win," insisted Mimi.

Fred the handyman was the judge every year. He dimmed the lights. It made the lobby look like a tomb. Soon everyone was very quiet.

Everyone except Maxi. The little rock star was standing by the elevator, barking like his life depended on it.

"What's the matter with him?" the strawberry shake asked the credit card.

Soon Mandy and Mimi and everybody else could see a huge shadow on the lobby wall, the very same shadow the friends had seen in the basement. It had the same wide shoulders and it was choking something round under its arm.

"The head!" screamed Mandy.

"The monster!" screamed Mimi.

The friends M and M were sure somebody would call the police.

"Join the party!" cried Fred to the monster. Mandy and Mimi couldn't believe their ears.

At that, the monster turned around. The creepy shadow left the wall as the monster came closer.

Then Fred made the lights bright.

Now everyone could see the monster standing there.

"Why, it's that nice new boy who just moved in," said Mrs. Haite, going for some punch.

"I let him borrow my bicycle chain," said the woman from upstairs. "He has such a nice bike."

"I found some leftover paint for him," said Godzilla's owner. "He's painting old crates for his new room. Red."

Suddenly Mandy and Mimi found themselves face to face with the monster. But the monster was a kid just like them. He wore a baggy brown football uniform a lot because he was trying out for a school team. His helmet was tucked under his arm.

"You live on 2," said the new kid to Mandy. "And I've seen you walk up one floor to 3," he told Mimi. "I use the back stairs a lot. They're faster. I'm new on 13."

"Thirteen must be your lucky number," Mimi mumbled.

"It's our cage number, too," said the new kid, whose name was Marco.

"We know," said Mandy.

Then Marco explained how he'd set up cage number 13 like a workshop. He kept his bike there, and painted things for his room.

"The basement's a great place," he went on. "It's quiet and your parents don't bother you. Maybe you'd like to visit the basement with me sometime?"

"Sure," said M and M together. Maybe they'd been wrong about basements, and a lot of other things.

Maxi won the prize for Best Costume. Everyone cheered for Maxi the rock star.

After the party, Mandy and Mimi and Marco played trick-or-treat on everyone in the building who would open their door to a strawberry milkshake, a BIG SPENDER credit card, a punk rock star, and a football player.

That night, Mandy and Mimi had a sleepover at Mimi's. Before they went to sleep, they gave Maxi a bath to get the sticky stuff out. Then they made marshmallow ghosts, and ate them all. They folded their costumes and put them away to save them forever.

"It was just a game," said Mimi. "All the scary things." Mandy agreed.

Then they fluffed up their pillows, and pulled the covers tight—just in case.

Don't miss Mandy and Mimi's
other adventures in:

Meet M and M
M and M and the Big Bag
M and M and the Bad News Babies
M and M and the Santa Secrets
M and M and the Mummy Mess
M and M and the Super Child Afternoon
M and M and the Haunted House Game